I LOVE
DOGS

by Tessa Kenan

BUMBA BOOKS™

LERNER PUBLICATIONS ◆ MINNEAPOLIS

Note to Educators:

Throughout this book, you'll find critical thinking questions. These can be used to engage young readers in thinking critically about the topic and in using the text and photos to do so.

Lerner Publications Company
A division of Lerner Publishing Group, Inc.
241 First Avenue North
Minneapolis, MN 55401 USA

For reading levels and more information, look up this title at www.lernerbooks.com.

Library of Congress Cataloging-in-Publication Data

Names: Kenan, Tessa, author.
Title: I love dogs / by Tessa Kenan.
Description: Minneapolis : Lerner Publications, [2017] | Series: Bumba books—Pets are the best | Audience: Ages 4–8. | Audience: K to grade 3. | Includes bibliographical references and index.
Identifiers: LCCN 2016001061 (print) | LCCN 2016004369 (ebook) | ISBN 9781512414141 (lb : alk. paper) | ISBN 9781512415193 (pb : alk. paper) | ISBN 9781512415209 (eb pdf)
Subjects: LCSH: Dogs—Juvenile literature.
Classification: LCC SF426.5 .K46 2017 (print) | LCC SF426.5 (ebook) | DDC 636.7/0887—dc23

LC record available at http://lccn.loc.gov/2016001061

Manufactured in the United States of America
2-45432-21342-2/21/2018

Expand learning beyond the printed book. Download free, complementary educational resources for this book from our website, www.lernerresource.com.

Table of Contents

Pet Dogs

Today we got a dog.

Dogs are pets.

We take good care

of our pets.

A collar fits around a dog's neck.

We buy a tag.

It shows the dog's name.

Why do we give our dog a name?

Dogs need to eat
each day.

We feed dogs special
dog food.

Dogs also need fresh
water.

Dogs need to exercise.

We take our dog on a walk.

We find fun ways to play

and move.

How else could your dog play and move?

We train dogs.

We can teach dogs to sit.

Dogs can learn to fetch.

Dogs can also learn tricks.

We reward dogs with treats.

We groom dogs.

We brush their fur.

We clip their nails.

We wash our pet dogs too.

Pet dogs go to a
veterinarian once a year.
A veterinarian is a
pet doctor.
She checks a dog's
health.
She helps sick dogs.

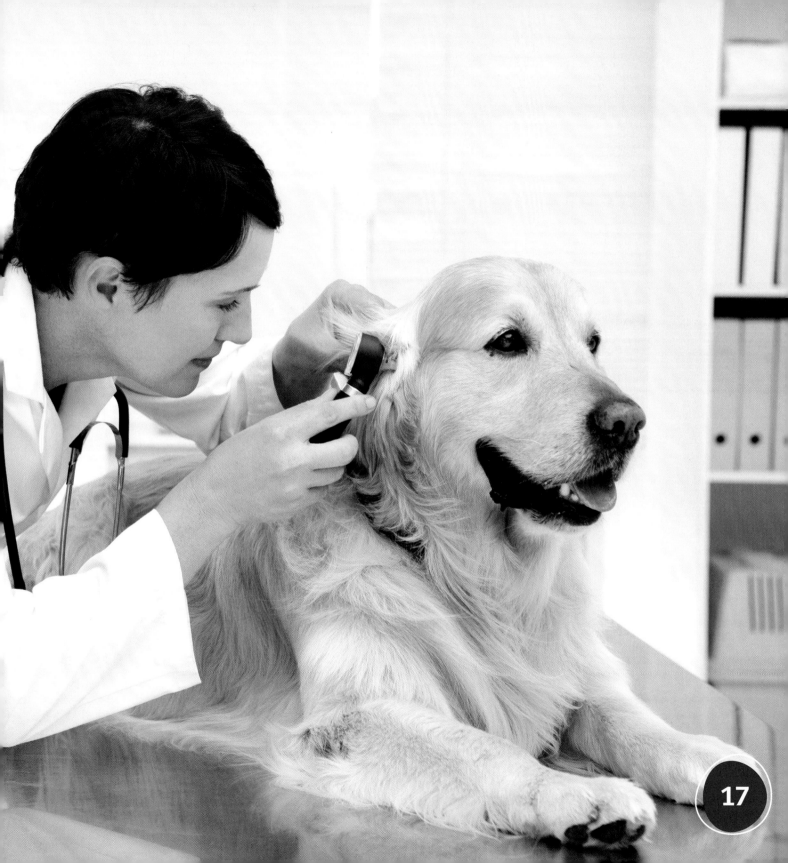

At night, dogs sleep in dog beds or kennels.

They rest after playing all day.

Why do you think some dogs sleep in kennels?

Pet dogs make great friends.

We love taking care of our dog.

Dog Supplies

dog bed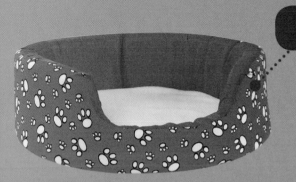

leash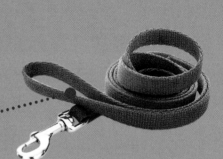

brush

kennel

water and food dish

collar

tag

Picture Glossary

exercise

moving and playing to stay healthy

groom

to brush and clean an animal

kennels

shelters that hold dogs

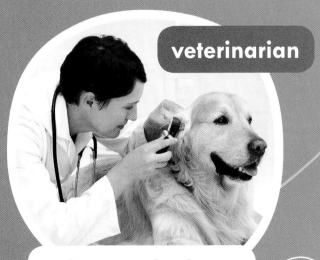

veterinarian

a doctor who is trained to treat sick or hurt animals

Index

Read More

Gaines, Ann. *Kids Top 10 Pet Dogs.* Berkeley Heights, NJ: Enslow Publishers, 2015.

Meister, Cari. *Dogs.* Minneapolis: Bullfrog Books, 2015.

Zobel, Derek. *Caring for Your Dog.* Minneapolis: Bellwether Media, 2010.

Photo Credits